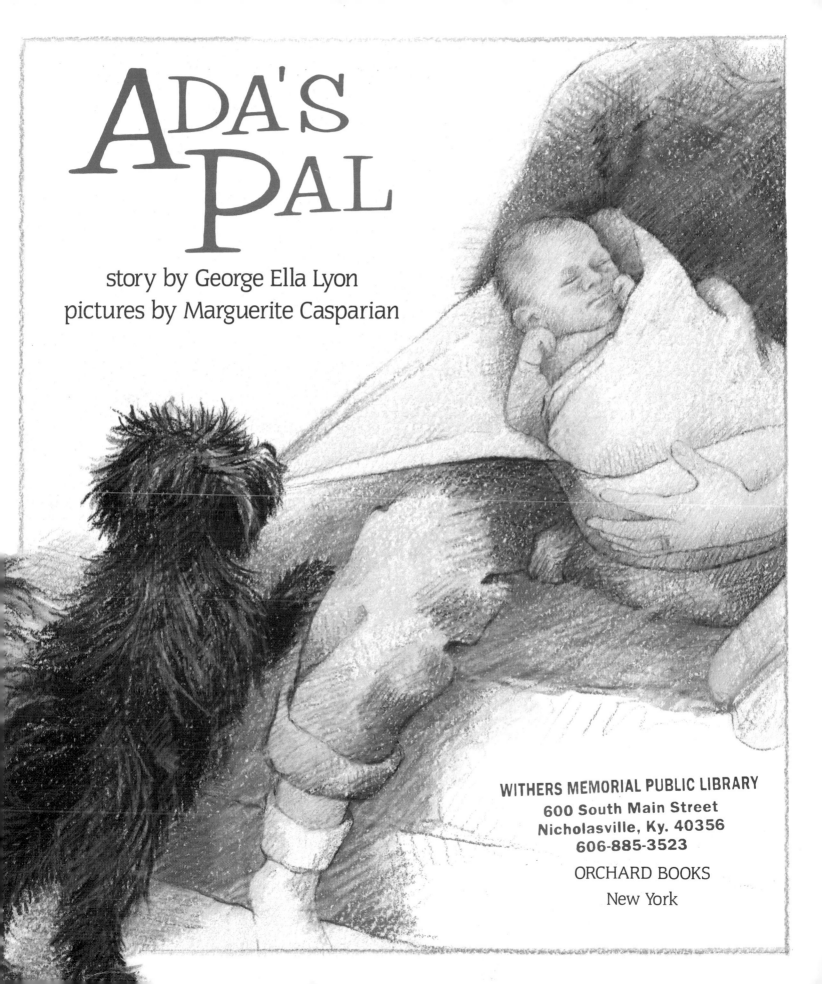

ADA'S PAL

story by George Ella Lyon
pictures by Marguerite Casparian

ORCHARD BOOKS
New York

Orchard Books, 95 Madison Avenue, New York, NY 10016

Manufactured in the United States of America
Printed by Barton Press, Inc. Bound by Horowitz/Rae
Book design by Jean Krulis
The text of this book is set in 16 point Congress Medium.
The illustrations are colored pencil and watercolor reproduced in full color.

10 9 8 7 6 5 4 3 2 1

Library of Congress Cataloging-in-Publication Data
Lyon, George Ella, date.
Ada's pal / story by George Ella Lyon; pictures by Marguerite Casparian.
p.   cm.
"A Richard Jackson book"—Half t.p.
Summary: A small dog suffers from a broken heart when her dog companion
dies until a veterinarian advises the family that there is only one thing to do.
ISBN 0-531-09528-2. — ISBN 0-531-08878-2 (lib. bdg.)
1. Dogs—Juvenile fiction. [1. Dogs—Fiction. 2. Death—Fiction.
3. Friendship—Fiction.] I. Casparian, Marguerite, ill. II. Title.
PZ10.3.L9875Ad   1996   [E]—dc20   95-53732

For my neighbor, Linda Potter, who shared her story,
and for Marguerite, my pal
—G.E.L.

For Peter and Rachel and Hannah—my pals
—M.C.

My first word was not Ma-ma

not Da-da

not even Bye-bye

but Ada.

Ada is our dog
   a black mop-without-a-handle dog
   just my size when I was crawling.
   I was her best friend

till we got Troublesome.

Troublesome was your big
knock-the-mail-carrier-down dog.
She had to stay in the backyard
so Ada whined to move out too.

Troublesome could
   chase squirrels
   bury bones
   bark at cars—
   stuff I couldn't do.
   She could chase Ada.

Ada spun around the yard
        like a wild wind-up toy
        with Troublesome leaping and starting
        with Troublesome yipping
        and slinging her ears

for years.

They howled and played and dreamed
side by side.

Then Troublesome got sick
    and no matter what she ate
    or what pills and shots the vet gave her
    she just got sicker.
    Finally she died.

We buried her in the yard
with her rawhide bone
beside the daisies she liked to lie in.

Mom picked Ada up and brought her in the house.

"Come on, girl," she said.

"We've still got you—

  still got someone to feed and pet and play with."

But Ada wasn't playing.
She lay in a corner
of the family room.

"Hey, Ada, let's go for a walk!"

"Here's your dog biscuit."

"Come on, girl. Fetch!"

She didn't move.

Dad said,

"It's being in the house
that does this."

So I opened the door
and carried Ada out.
She stood exactly where I set her.
"Go on," I said, and touched her head.
She sank to the ground.

"Do you think she's sick like Troublesome?
Do you think she'll die too?"

The vet just said,
"Give it time."

The next day Ada wet the kitchen floor.

She didn't run and hide.

She lay down in the puddle.

"Time's up," Mom said.

Ada was like a ragdoll
while Dr. Carey checked her.
She didn't whimper when he drew blood.

"Nothing wrong with this dog but a broken heart."

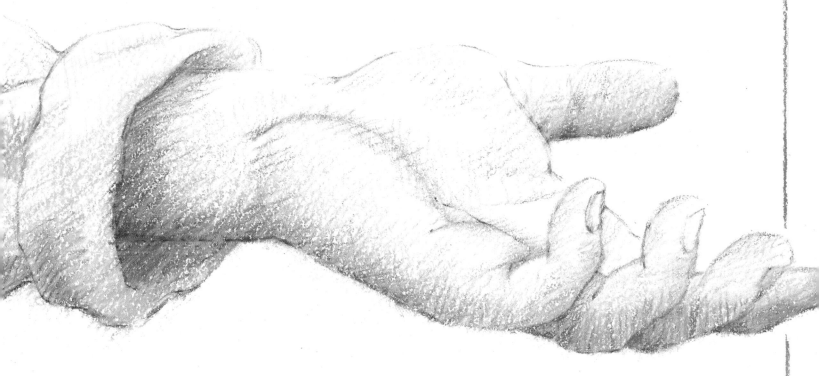

"Maybe a pill?" I asked.

He shook his head.

I said, "I think what Ada needs is a dog."

So we took the long way home
around by the animal shelter.

In the first room, the third cage
we found a golden pup.
Palomino, I call him. Pal, for short.

Ada *did not like it*
when we put Pal in the car.

She growled all the way home.

When Mom took Pal in the house
Ada stayed in the yard.

She went to the food dish.
She went to the gate.
She stood perfectly still.
Then she howled a long, shivery howl.

It must have made her hungry
because later she ate a little.

She slept outside by the gate.

When I put Pal out this morning

Ada barked
    Pal bounded
Ada barked harder
    Pal ran
Ada became a blizzard of barks.

She covered the whole yard
with Pal right behind her.
He thought she was playing

and pretty soon she was.

They chased each other all day,

spent all night side by side.

Mom says now we know
a dog's best friend is a dog.